AQUA DOG

BY LISA VAN DER WIELEN
ILLUSTRATED BY ALISON MUTTON

FOR ANDY
LISA VAN DER WIELEN

ABOUT THE AUTHOR

Lisa Van Der Wielen is a children's author and primary school teacher from Perth, Western Australia. Her passion for teaching and writing lead her to publish her first picture book, *Vegetarian Polony*, in 2017. *Luna Lucy* was published in 2018, followed by a sequel, *Luna Lucy and the Planets* in 2019, along with *Aqua Dog* and *Gus*. The importance of virtues, and Lisa's love for the beach, nature, dogs and family inspire her to write fun rhyming tales that encourage children to learn, laugh and enjoy the magic of reading.

ABOUT THE ILLUSTRATOR

Alison Mutton is an illustrator from Perth, Western Australia. She graduated from Curtin University with a Bachelor of Design (Hons) majoring in Illustration, in 2008 and has been working in the children's and educational publishing fields ever since. When not illustrating, she enjoys walking her dog Myrna, playing the piano and needle felting.

Aqua Dog

First published March 2019

Text © Lisa Van Der Wielen 2019
Illustrations © Alison Mutton / Alene Illustration 2019

The moral rights of the author and illustrator have been asserted,

Typeset in Gentona and Stupidhead
Graphic Design: Alison Mutton

Alene Illustration
www.alene-art.com

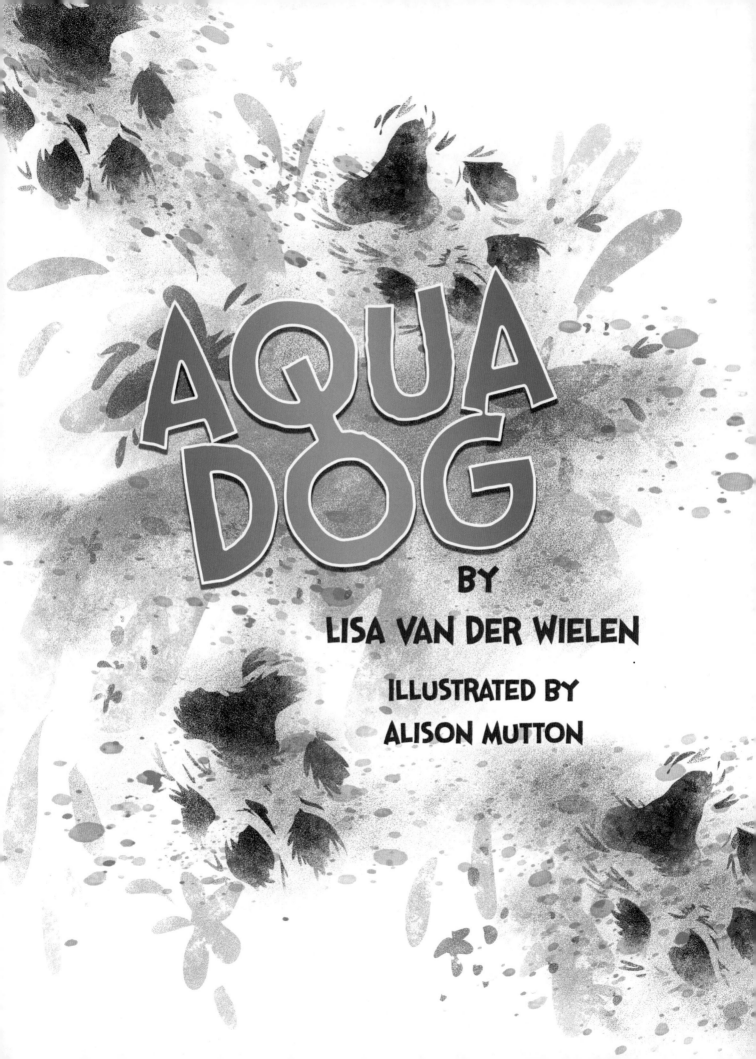

AQUA DOG

BY

LISA VAN DER WIELEN

ILLUSTRATED BY

ALISON MUTTON

Down on the farm lived an aquatic hound.
Who learnt to swim since rescued from the pound.

From the time he could dig, he could swim like a fish.
He'd dive down deep, with a
SPLASH and a SPLISH.

Aqua would swim every single day.
Splashing around was his favourite play.

The farmer got angry when he'd dive down deep.
Instead of running around, herding up the sheep.

"AQUA," he'd yell,
"GET OUT OF THAT DAM!
GO AND HERD SHEEP, AND CHASE THAT LAMB!"

So Aqua would go and do as he was told.
But what he wanted to do was swim 'til cold.

Then one very stormy day, the farm filled with rain.
Covering the animals, the crops and the grain.

The farm got flooded, the water got deep.
The levels were rising above the sheep.

"**HELP!**" cried the farmer,
"THE ANIMALS MIGHT DROWN.
WE NEED TO GET THEM SAFE,
TO THE HIGH END OF TOWN!"

Then out of his kennel, splashed man's best friend.
Barking in bubbles,

"ON ME YOU CAN DEPEND!"

So Aqua did the thing he did best:
He swam and he swam to save the rest.

HE PADDLED

AND GLIDED;

HE DIVED

AND HE STROKED

He saved the sheep,
who were very stoked

But just when he thought his swimming was profound –
He looked for the farmer,
but heard not a sound.

He barked with bubbles,
he sang like a whale.
He dove down deep,
with the flick of his tail.

For below the water, the farmer couldn't swim.
LUCKY AQUA THE DOG WAS THERE TO RESCUE HIM.

He pulled the farmer to safety and dragged him to higher ground.
Where the farmer lay there, grateful and spellbound.

"THANK YOU," he whispered to his furry friend.
"FOREVER I'LL BE GLAD, FOR YOUR SWIMMING TREND."

Once the flood subsided, and the water disappeared.
The farm was all messy and had to be cleared.

The farm looked different;
SOMETHING SPECIAL HAD BEEN BUILT
for a remarkable dog, out of a
farmer's guilt.

"I'VE BUILT YOU SOMETHING SPECIAL,
YOU CLEVER LITTLE TYKE.
A WAY TO SAY THANK YOU THAT I HOPE YOU WILL LIKE..."

Out in the paddock was a glistening, blue pool.
But before Aqua the dog could even drool –

He ran and jumped in,

SPLISH

SPLOSH

SPLASH!

Under the water he went in a flash.

Aqua dog was a hero, with a smile from ear to ear.
He had his own swimming pool, to use throughout the year!

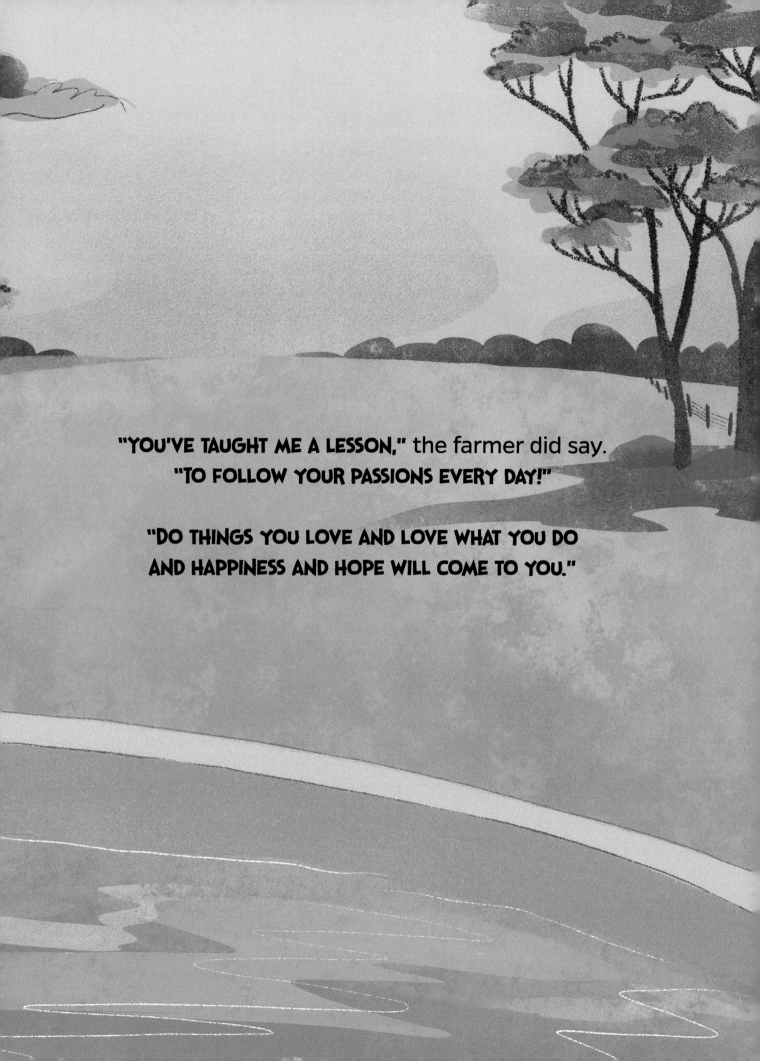

"YOU'VE TAUGHT ME A LESSON," the farmer did say.
"TO FOLLOW YOUR PASSIONS EVERY DAY!"

**"DO THINGS YOU LOVE AND LOVE WHAT YOU DO
AND HAPPINESS AND HOPE WILL COME TO YOU."**

Made in the USA
Middletown, DE
20 December 2021

56678691R00018